THE LUNATIC ADVENTURE OF

KITMAN AND WILLY

BY CHRIS L. DEMAREST

SIMON AND SCHUSTER BOOKS FOR YOUNG READERS
PUBLISHED BY SIMON & SCHUSTER INC., NEW YORK

TO

WHIT STILLMAN

SIMON AND SCHUSTER BOOKS FOR YOUNG READERS
Simon & Schuster Building
Rockefeller Center
1230 Avenue of the Americas
New York, New York 10020

Manufactured in the United States of America
Hand lettering by Anthony Bloch

10 9 8 7 6 5 4 3 2 1

Library of Congress Cataloging in Publication Data
Demarest, Chris L. The lunatic adventure of Kitman and Willy. Summary: Kitman and Willy's adventures take them into space, where they dislodge
the moon and several stars from their places and have to think of a way of putting them back. [1. Interplanetary voyages—Fiction]
I. Title. PZ7.D3914Lw   1988   [E]   87-32354
ISBN 0-671-65695-3

"IT'S A WONDERFUL NIGHT FOR AN ADVENTURE," THOUGHT KITMAN AND WILLY, "BUT WHAT CAN WE DO?"

THEY THOUGHT VERY HARD — SO HARD THAT WILLY'S HEAD BEGAN TO HURT.
"I KNOW," KITMAN CRIED OUT, "WE'LL GO TO THE MOON."

"YEAH!" SHOUTED WILLY. "THAT'S TERRIFIC."

OFF THEY RACED TO BEGIN THEIR ADVENTURE.

IN NO TIME THEY WERE READY. "FIRST, WE TAKE THIS ROCK..." EXPLAINED KITMAN.

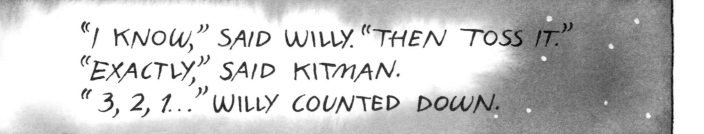

"I KNOW," SAID WILLY. "THEN TOSS IT."
"EXACTLY," SAID KITMAN.
" 3, 2, 1..." WILLY COUNTED DOWN.

WHOOSH! UP INTO THE AIR THEY STREAKED.
HIGHER AND HIGHER.

BUT NOT HIGH ENOUGH. AS QUICKLY AS THEY HAD RISEN, THEY FELL.

SUDDENLY A SHOOTING STAR RACED TOWARD THEM, AND KITMAN AND WILLY GRABBED ON.

UP AND DOWN, AROUND AND AROUND THEY FLEW, SNATCHING AT EVERY STAR THEY PASSED, TRYING TO SLOW DOWN.

CRASH! KITMAN AND WILLY STRUCK THE MOON. DOWN THEY ALL TUMBLED.

"OH NO," SAID KITMAN RUBBING HIS HEAD.
"NOW WHAT HAVE WE DONE?"
WILLY JUST STARED.

"HOW," THEY BOTH WONDERED, "WILL WE PUT THE STARS AND THE MOON BACK WHERE THEY BELONG?" SUDDENLY, KITMAN HAD AN IDEA.

"IT'S VERY SIMPLE," HE EXPLAINED TO THE MOON. THE MOON AGREED.

AND WITH ONE BIG LEAP ALL THE STARS
SAILED HOME.

BUT THAT LEFT ONE PROBLEM.
"I DON'T KNOW WHAT TO DO," SIGHED KITMAN.
WILLY SEEMED JUST AS CONFUSED.

"WE'LL HAVE YOU ON YOUR WAY IN NO TIME," CHUCKLED WILLY.

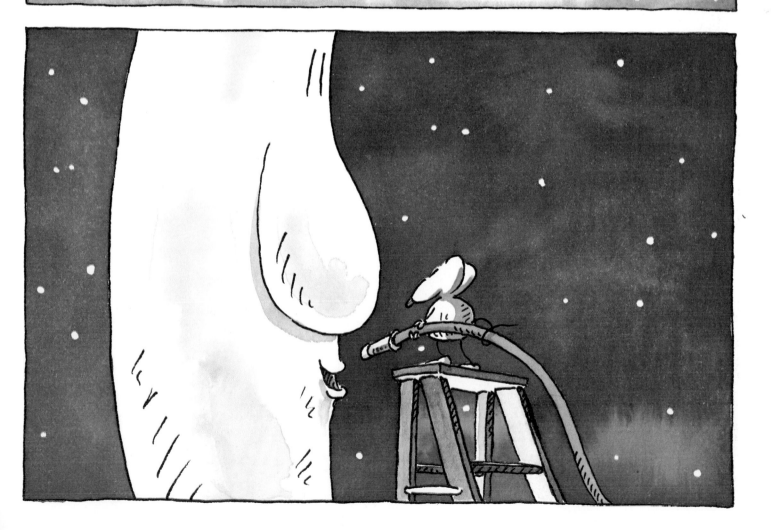

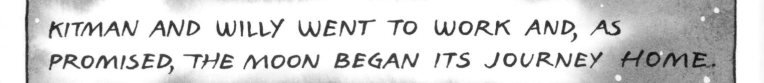

KITMAN AND WILLY WENT TO WORK AND, AS PROMISED, THE MOON BEGAN ITS JOURNEY HOME.

WITH THE MOON BEAMING DOWN UPON THEM, KITMAN AND WILLY PLANNED THEIR NEXT ADVENTURE.